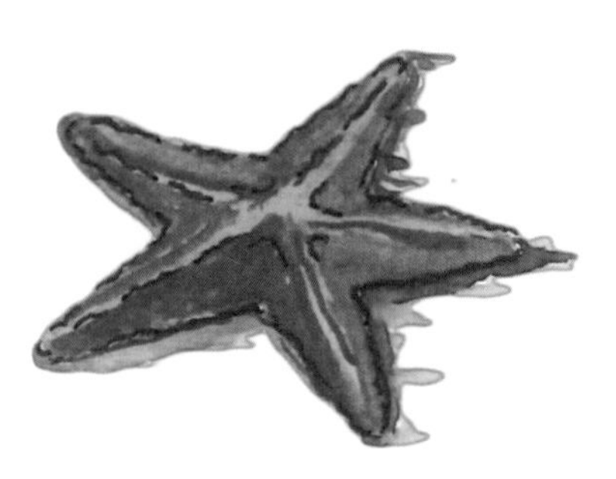

This book belongs to:

....

With thanks to Jessica Taylor for marine biology consultancy, Cinque Port Printing for image scanning, Steven Blackery for artistic support, Peter Glass for assistance with image editing and our families for endless encouragement.

Published by Sartain Publishing Ltd, London
www.sartainpublishing.co.uk

ISBN 978-1-9996292-2-9

Emma Rosen

Evgeniia Blackery

Lily the Limpet Gets Lost

Down on the beach in Littletown Bay,
Between sea and sand, rocks stand in the way.
When the sea flows out, as it does with each tide,
You'll see, as it goes, it leaves rock pools behind.
Each dip in the stone, each gully and gap,
Is filled with saltwater that has become trapped.
In each little pool, if you take care and look,
There are lots of small creatures in every small nook.

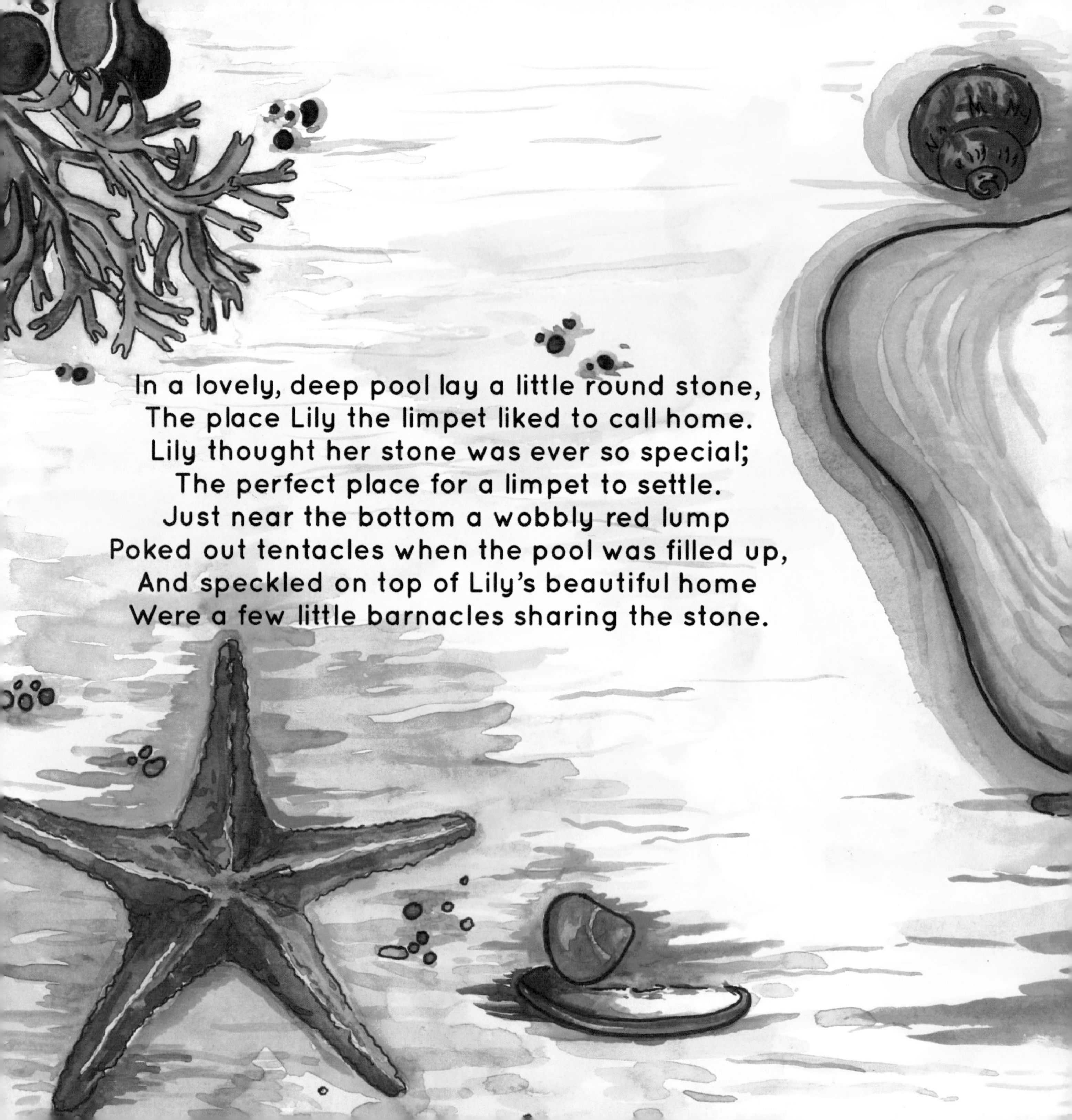

In a lovely, deep pool lay a little round stone,
The place Lily the limpet liked to call home.
Lily thought her stone was ever so special;
The perfect place for a limpet to settle.
Just near the bottom a wobbly red lump
Poked out tentacles when the pool was filled up,
And speckled on top of Lily's beautiful home
Were a few little barnacles sharing the stone.

The pool emptied a little when water left with the tide,
But Lily never worried about getting too dry.
She would cling to the rock as tight as could be
So from her shell no water would leak.

She had lived on that stone almost since she was born,
And just where she rested a circle was worn.
Her shell fitted perfectly onto her spot
And so she never lost so much as a drop.

The pool was still full; Lily could tell.
She loosened her foot and looked out from her shell .

She peeped all around, making sure she was safe
To slip from her stone and see what had changed.
Lily looked round. She fancied a bite.
She wanted to lick some rocks that taste nice.

She started to slither around in her pool,
Her rough tongue scraping small plants from the walls.

Billy clung to Gran's hand as he climbed on the rocks;
His bucket filled with water halfway to the top.
Gran had a little net just for the fish,
And she told him, "Look out for the seaweed! Don't slip."
Billy's Granny pointed to this and to that.
They collected a shell and a scurrying crab.
Then, at the bottom of a beautiful pool,
Billy spotted a stone. He reached in and he pulled.

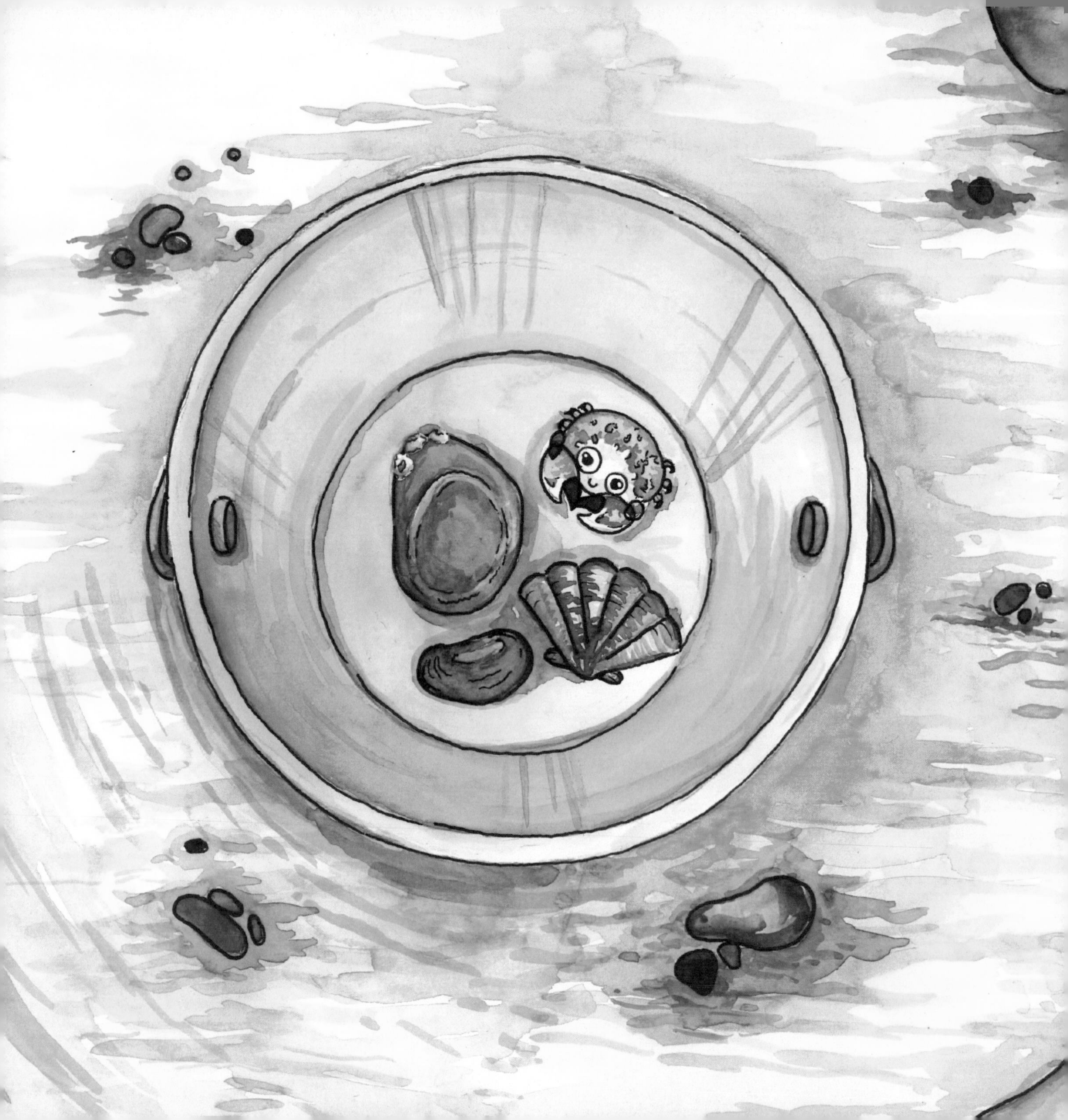

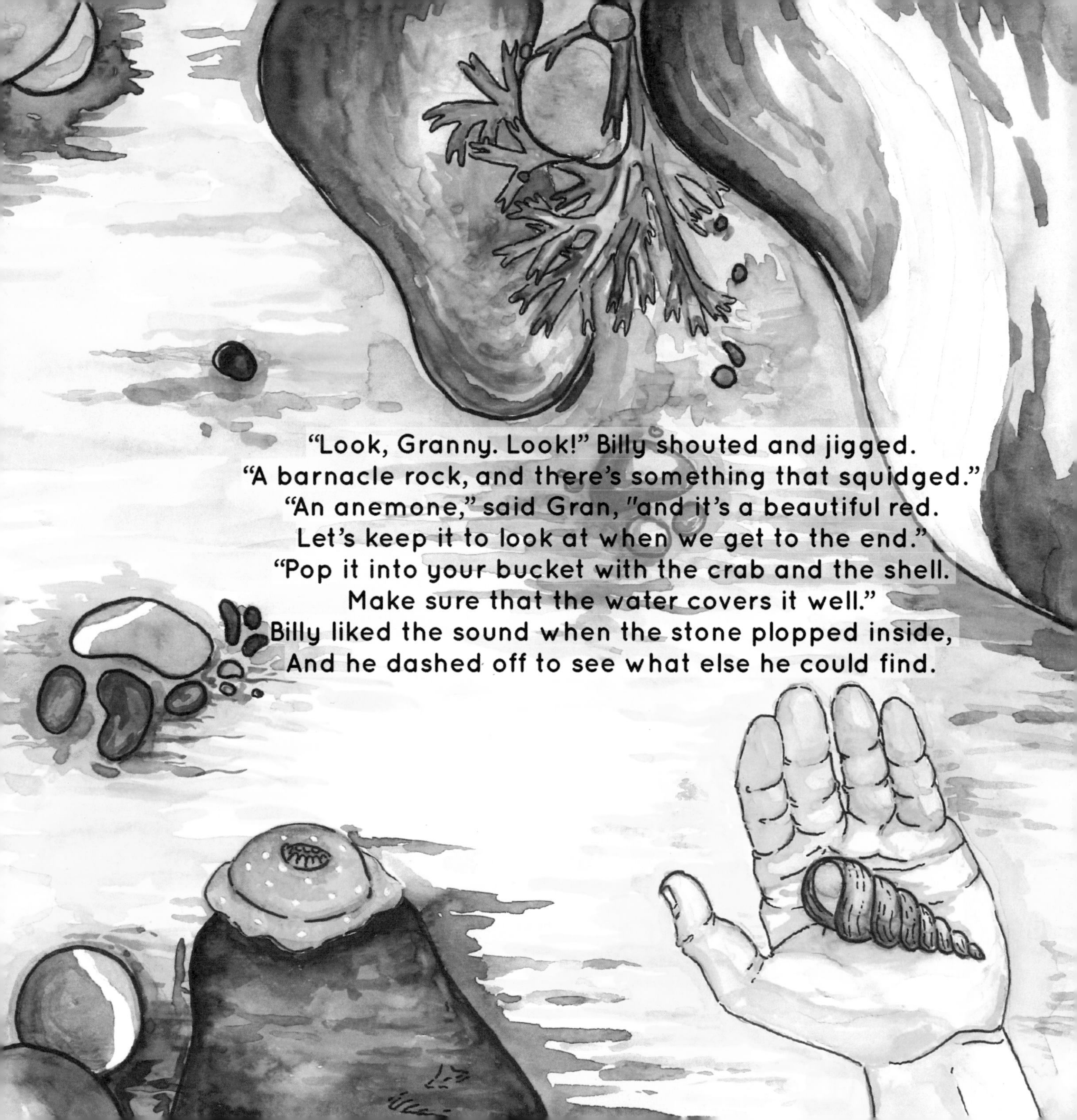

"Look, Granny. Look!" Billy shouted and jigged.
"A barnacle rock, and there's something that squidged."
"An anemone," said Gran, "and it's a beautiful red.
Let's keep it to look at when we get to the end."
"Pop it into your bucket with the crab and the shell.
Make sure that the water covers it well."
Billy liked the sound when the stone plopped inside,
And he dashed off to see what else he could find.

Lily didn't like to wander too far,
And her tummy was full of tiny green plants.
She started to slither back to her home
Where she could wait for the tide and rest on her stone.

Oh no! What was this? Her trail stopped short.
It didn't loop back to her home like it ought.
Where was the stone? Where were her friends?
Where was the spot where her trail always ends?

Lily checked all along her trail from today
Just in case somehow she'd got lost on the way.
She slithered all round the outside of the pool,
Then checked in the middle, but saw nothing at all.
"Have you seen my stone?" Lily asked a small fish.
"Have you seen my stone?" she questioned a shrimp.
"Oh, where is my stone?" Lily started to cry.
It seemed to have gone and she didn't know why.

A starfish crawled out from a patch of green weed.
"You look lost," it said and Lily agreed.
Then Lily looked up and saw who she'd heard speak,
"Starfish eat limpets," she said with a squeak.
Quick as a flash she pushed her shell up.
Standing tall like a mushroom she hoped for some luck.
When her shell was over one of the starfish's legs
She stamped on it hard and then, quickly, she fled.

Lily was scared; she didn't know what to do.
Where could she go, except the spot where she grew?
She wouldn't stick on sand or fit on the rocks
And the water could vanish if the day got too hot.
A starfish was near who could eat her for tea,
And if a wave crashed she could be washed out to sea!
Most of all she missed her friends from the stone:
The anemone and the barnacles that shared her home.

Granny and Billy sat down by the sea.
Billy peered into the bucket squealing with glee.
"We found so much, Granny, as we followed the tide:
The crab, shell and rock. I love the seaside!"

"Now Billy," said Gran, "I'm glad you had fun,
But there's one thing to do before we are done.
Everything here must go back in the sea.
That's where they're safe and where they should be."

Billy was careful when he put the
things back.
Gran helped him figure out just
where they'd sat:
The shell in some seaweed, the crab
under a ledge
And the stone in a deep pool just
near the edge.

The splash of the stone made Lily's heart race.
She turned, and her stone was back in its place.
Lily climbed on and with relief closed her eyes
While, stuck to her rock, she awaited the tide.

Lightning Source UK Ltd.
Milton Keynes UK
UKRC020042040919
349142UK00006B/36

* 9 7 8 1 9 9 9 6 2 9 2 2 9 *